His Mother's Dog

HARPER & ROW, PUBLISHERS
New York, Hagerstown, London, San Francisco

Weekly Reader Books presents

His Mother's Dog

by Liesel Moak Skorpen

Pictures by M. E. Mullin

HIS MOTHER'S DOG

Text copyright © 1978 by Liesel Moak Skorpen

Illustrations copyright © 1978 by M. E. Mullin

Library of Congress Cataloging in Publication Data
Skorpen, Liesel Moak.
  His mother's dog.

  SUMMARY: A young boy is disappointed when his puppy follows his mother everywhere, but the situation changes with the advent of a new baby.
  [1. Dogs—Fiction] I. Mullin, Mary Ellen.
II. Title.
PZ7.S62837Hi   [E]   76-58707
ISBN 0-06-025722-9
ISBN 0-06-025723-7 lib. bdg.

For the Juergens
Great and small
George and Jane
Steve and Paul

He woke up early because his feet were cold.

It had snowed all night and he couldn't see where the driveway was supposed to be. He'd have to shovel out. A big, orange plow rumbled along, clearing the road for the school buses. So he got dressed, and without waking anyone up, shoveled as much snow as he could manage and brought in a good load of wood for the kitchen fire.

His mother was surprised and very pleased. "It must be the first time in your life," she said, slicing the bread, "you've ever done something like that without being told to. And you know," she said, smiling and pouring the hot chocolate, "I think you might be old enough to have that dog for your birthday this year, if you still want a dog."

He wanted a dog.
He had always wanted a dog.

His father wasn't so sure it was a good idea. "A dog is a lot of responsibility," he said, frowning. "A dog is not a toy—not like that silly racing set you had to have last year. You can't play with a dog for a while and then forget it."

He knew that a dog was not a toy.
He had always wanted a dog.

11

The dog book from the library showed all the sorts of dogs there are all over the world. There were little dogs without enough hair. There were little dogs with too much hair. There were large, lean dogs with too many teeth. Right away he liked the Newfoundlands. "They're almost as big as ponies," he said, pleased. His mother was looking at the cocker spaniels. She'd had a cocker spaniel when she was a girl.

"I guess I'll get a Newfoundland," he said.
"Too big," said his father. "They eat too much."
"I'll give him my leftovers," he said.
They pretty well promised he could have a dog,
but not necessarily a Newfoundland.

Right away he could see it wasn't a Newfoundland.
For one bad moment he thought it might be one of those dogs without enough hair. It was a cocker spaniel pup with large, soft, worried eyes and a short, cheerful tail.

Right away he liked the little dog.
Right away the little dog liked his mother.

He named the dog Moose, because that was the name he'd been saving. "That's cute," said his mother, trying to sound cheerful. The dog his mother used to have was Puck. Sometimes she called the puppy Puck by mistake. Sometimes she called the puppy Puck on purpose, and after a while everyone called it Puck and nobody called it Moose anymore.

Wherever his mother went, her dog liked to go with her, except when she went somewhere in the car. And then her dog sat in the window chair and watched the cars go by.

When his mother went upstairs, her dog went up.
When his mother went down, down came her dog.
When his mother was cooking something in the kitchen,
her dog stayed under the table,
watching her feet go by.
Whenever she whistled or called,
the dog came running.
Whenever he whistled or called,
the dog went to look for his mother.
At night the dog slept on the floor
by his mother's door.

He fed the dog three times a day and took it out early in the morning, before anyone else was up, and late at night, after everyone else was in bed. The dog never wanted to go out with him. It always wanted to stay where his mother was. It didn't like snow and it didn't like rain or blustery winds, or fog, or funny noises. It would sit at the end of its leash and stare at the ground, waiting for him to give up and take it in. Then it would make a mess by his father's chair, and his father would be mad at him because he was supposed to be responsible and because it was his dog.

One Saturday his father said he had something important to talk to him about. Right away he figured he was in trouble. And all the way up the meadow and into the woods, he was trying to remember what he'd done. His mother's dog followed them a little while, but then it ran back to the house to look for his mother. They sat on a rock where they sometimes used to sit when he was little. His father said they were going to have a baby. He said they had always wanted another child, so they were very happy. His father put his arm around him.

It was hard to see why his mother would want a baby.
She already had a dog.
He didn't want a baby.
He had never wanted a baby.
But he didn't tell his father or his mother.
He didn't want to spoil things for them.

It was a girl.

His grandmother came to stay while his mother was in the hospital. He'd always liked his grandmother. She had special games and puzzles for him at her house and good desserts. But at his house she was bossy and she made him eat soft-boiled eggs and whole wheat toast, and he overheard her telling his father that he was spoiled and badly brought up.

His mother's dog sat in the window chair.
It wouldn't eat anything—not even hamburgers.

His father and his grandmother were very pleased about the baby. His father kept saying "your sister." "Your sister weighs more than you did—seven pounds, ten ounces." "Your sister's eyes are blue, and it looks like her hair is going to be fair like her mother's."

He didn't care what colors his fat sister was.
He missed his mother.

She took him in her arms and hugged and hugged him.
His father was holding the baby.

His mother looked fine—just like she used to look. It felt like
everything would be all right, but then the baby began to
whimper, and his mother said, "Oh dear, she must be
hungry," and hurried off to feed her.

He was thinking how happy his mother's dog would be to
see his mother again. His grandmother, who didn't like dogs,
had tied it out behind the barn.

His mother was in the bedroom nursing the baby. He was right—her dog was very happy to see her. It ran in circles around her chair, barking with delight and wagging all over.

The baby made a mewing noise.
His mother's dog stopped in its tracks.
Its ruff went up.
It backed away, growling and baring its teeth.
His mother was screaming.
The baby was screaming.
His father was furious.
"What an idiot trick to play!" he said.
His mother's dog had to stay outside most of the time.
"Puck's so jealous," his mother said.
"He might be dangerous."

The baby's name was Rebecca. He would have named her Moose if he'd been asked, but nobody asked him. Everyone thought she was wonderful because she slept a lot and almost never cried. His grandmother was so busy admiring the baby, she didn't have time to boss him around. So he had jelly doughnuts and root beer for breakfast. She forgot to say "good-by" when she went home.

The house was always quiet. His mother and her baby were always taking naps. His father had told him not to make any noise before he went off in the car somewhere. He'd been working on a puzzle with too many pieces missing, when all of a sudden he just felt like singing. Singing wasn't noise. What he felt like singing was something nice and loud. He found some cookie sheets that made good cymbals.

His mother's door opened.
She looked mad and sleepy.
"Outside," she said, pointing to the door,
"before you wake your sister!"

He sat on the steps beside his mother's dog.
His mother's dog was staring at the door,
hoping his mother might want it to come in.

He decided to take a walk.
Maybe he'd take a good, long walk.
Maybe he'd never come back.

He was over the field, well into the wood, when he noticed
his mother's dog was following him. It wasn't very close and
it wasn't coming closer. When he got tired of walking and
turned for home, his mother's dog turned too.

His mother had warmed him up a frozen dinner.
He hated frozen dinners.
"Isn't there any homemade bread?" he said.
His mother looked as if she were going to cry. She said she had just had a baby and just come home from the hospital and what did he expect.

Her eyes were angry.
Her voice was hard—
as if she didn't love him anymore.
He said he wasn't hungry and he went upstairs.

He lay on his bed with his hands behind his head. He was thinking that what he'd like to do was to live by himself in a forest somewhere else—he'd just have a dog, a good, big dog, a Newfoundland, for company, and he'd eat wild berries and maybe make friends with wild bears—when he heard a little scratching on his door. The door pushed open just enough to let his mother's dog look in. "Get out of here, Stupid," he said, rolling over and burying his face in the

pillow. After quite a while, he took a peek just to be sure the dog was good and gone. The dog was sitting by his bed, staring down at its feet or at the floor.

"What's the matter, Moose?" he said softly.
"You look like you've lost your best friend."
He never meant to say that.
He never meant to cry.

His mother's dog was standing on his stomach, licking his
chin and his salty cheeks and his ears and the end of his
nose, and he was laughing because its cold tongue tickled,
and his mother's dog was wagging all over because it liked
his laugh.

Later his mother came in to say "good night."
She said that she was sorry.
He said he was sorry too.
She said she wasn't mad at him.

She said that she loved him with her whole heart
and always, always would.
Someday, she said, he might even like the baby.
He said he didn't think so, but he'd try.

After that, wherever he went, his mother's dog liked to go with him, except when he went somewhere on the school bus. And then it sat in the window chair, watching the bus go by.

When he went up, his mother's dog went up.

When he came down, down came his mother's dog.

Whenever he whistled, his mother's dog came running.

And because at night his mother's dog always wanted to be
where he was, it always slept at the end of his bed.
So even when it snowed all night,
his feet were never cold.